Who Will Guide My Sleigh Tonight?

Jerry Pallotta

David Biedrzycki

SCHOLASTIC INC.

New York   Toronto   London   Auckland   Sydney
Mexico City   New Delhi   Hong Kong   Buenos Aires

ISBN 0-439-38914-3

Text copyright © 2005 by Jerry Pallotta   Illustrations copyright © 2005 by David Biedrzycki   All rights reserved.
Published by Scholastic Inc.   SCHOLASTIC and associated logos are trademarks and/or registered trademarks of Scholastic Inc.

12 11 10 9 8 7 6 5 4 3 2   5 6 7 8 9 10/0

Printed in Singapore
First printing, November 2005

The job was too big for me. I needed help!

I had the sleigh. But one helper just wouldn't do.

I was looking for a team!

I tried tigers.

They played too rough. They almost ate me!

I tried mice.

They couldn't even lift the straps!

The penguins flapped and flapped.

Oops, they flipped and flopped!

The dolphins were really smart.

But—SPLASH!—they took me for a swim!

I loved the giraffes.

Oh! No! They got stuck.

I gave the skunks a try.

It was a smelly idea!

HOP! **HOP!** Kangaroos! HOP! HOP!

The HOP! presents HOP! went HOP! everywhere.

The turtles...

were...

The cheetahs were too fast.

Snakes! Snakes!

I tried rhinoceroses.

Bam! Crash! They smashed through a house!

"Don't even think about it!" said Mrs. Claus.

"Bunnies are for Easter."

I tried monkeys.

"Stop it! Don't look at my underwear!"

Then I had a bright idea!

Reindeer! That's it! They can do it all.

What a nice smooth ride! Yahoo!

Ho! Ho! Ho! Merry Christmas! Happy New Year!

Next year, maybe
I will try butterflies.

Ho! Ho! Ho! Merry Christmas! Happy New Year!

Next year, maybe
I will try butterflies.